Disclaimer

This is a work of fiction. Any names, businesses, characters, events, incidents and places are either the product of the author's imagination or used in a fictitious manner. Any resemblance to actual people, living or dead, or actual events or occurrences is purely coincidental.

A Mysterious Journey

The Bard's Tale
Book 1

By Blaine Hart
Copyright © 2016

Check Out all My Books and Audio Books at: www.LordHartRules.com

Table of Contents

Chapter 1 : The Witch Harpy of the North

There are stories still being whispered among the people of Theugua. Stories told about creatures hiding in the darkest corners of the world. Stories told about magic that could turn good and honest men against each other, stories about deeds that are darker than even the moonless night sky. Even so, men are quick to forget. Soon those hushed stories became nothing more than children's tales told in times of peace.

For Ornsell son of Krull, that was always the case. The stories of the past were just legends that would never come to pass. He decided to start his day early and head straight into the woods to check the traps he had set the day before. As he proceeded along at a brisk pace, getting back home in time for supper was his only concern. Handling his axe with ease, he set off towards the forest. He was also planning to cut some firewood that would last him and his son, Vygarast, for a week on his way back home.

Day excursions into the forest west of Midvein were ordinary for the village people. Though the winters up north of Theugua tended to be harsh and unforgiving, the men and women of Midvein were tough. They knew that the best way to survive the cold winds of the north was to be prepared for anything.

The morning dew had covered everything in the forest with a sparkling veil under the rising sun. Ornsell had his hands folded in front of him on his chest to try and keep himself warm. Taking a deep breath every five strides or so, he soon found himself deep in the woods and his exertions made the chill less now.

Winter mornings are the best remedy for an old man's head like mine. This is as good day as any to explore deeper into the forest, how many good days yet until I can't take a walk into the forest without needing Vygarast to help me? He laughed on the outside at the thought of being helped through the forest.

His eldest and only son was destined to be a Bard, one trained by a living legend, Lanarast the Bold. Being around to take care of him was not in his son's plans. *So be it!* He laughed it off. *If Vygarast's fate is to sing in the kings' courts and charm women with his voice for the rest of his life, then so be it.* However, a sudden frown and flush of emotion betrayed that thought. Memories of his life as a Bard (an amateur one that it was) kept interfering with his expectations for his talented young son.

You can't be jealous of your own son Ornsell. He has talent where you only had luck to rely on. Just get over it! With a quick shake of his head, he kept on heading deeper into the forest, sometimes choosing to follow the forest path, other times getting away from it. The forest was beautiful and full of life despite the chill. However, Ornsell could not get his son out of his mind. Lost in his own thoughts he ventured deeper into the woods. It was only after hearing a twig snap behind him that he jerked suddenly aware, his thoughts alarmed. He turned around only to see the dark shadows cast by the trees dance around him on the ground. Even if he couldn't see it, something felt wrong to him.

Bears are still asleep this late in the winter and it's too early into the day for the wolves to hunt. Normally, Ornsell was not a man who fretted over a dry twig snapping, but he couldn't shake the feeling that something, or someone, was following him.

A seasoned soldier, one matured in the last war of the Horizons, Ornsell wasn't afraid of any man bearing a sword, nor even some who cast magic. Nature was his only concern and by paying his respects to the Great Mother every spring, he didn't have anything to be afraid of. No, no matter how many times he thought about it, still something just wasn't right.

I hope Skann's boys are not in the mood for one of their pranks again or they're going have a day's worth of bottom ache when I finish with them. Those kids smell trouble from afar, especially since their father doesn't give them a good beating when they deserve it. Still, Ornsell went on, despite knowing quite well that a kid's prank would not leave such a vile sense in the back of his mind and that they would not dare venture this far into the forest alone.

Looking around, Ornsell suddenly realized that he had no idea where he was. The sun's bright rays barely crept between the leaves of the mighty evergreen and oak forest. Shadows were dancing as grey clouds passed above the thick forest. Cold sweat started to run down Ornsell's spine.

Whatever is following me can't be good. His left hand instinctively rested on the handle of his axe. Then he slowly pulled it out as his heart pounded fiercely in his chest. His brown eyes quickly examined his surroundings, trying to make out what had made that noise. Unaware of what was chasing him, he decided to follow his instincts and run. His warrior's sense of intuition, honed in the heat of the battle, was the only reason he was still alive after all of these years. The few times he didn't hear them, or he ignored them, he ended up in the back lines, limping and nursing his injuries.

Ornsell saw a break in the forest and took off, crashing through the forest for a full ten minutes, unable to spot anything in the dark behind him. The rustling of the fallen leaves being squashed under his boots became more apparent, and a few cracking twigs that he didn't break sent him jumping behind a large giant oak tree, noticing a terrible pain in his right ankle as he did so. His mind wasn't sure that something was actually following him, but his gut kept shouting a warning. *You have to run, old Orn, you have to run and hide!* With his right ankle aching badly he knew that the only way to get out of there alive was to either hide or fight.

He ran into a clearing amidst the dark woods. Ornsell knew that this place was his best chance for salvation. He was never one for hiding, especially not when he had a perfectly good axe in his right hand and solid ground beneath him. But he knew not to ignore his gut, so he brazenly ran towards the golden light of the still rising sun. Ornsell was sure he could sense the freezing breath of some vile creature on his neck. With desperation, Ornsell dove into the illuminating circle of the glade, landing roughly into a throng of black twigs and unearthed roots.

Gasping, he quickly stood on his feet once again. The warmth of the sun falling on his shoulder was relieving. Hungry for air, he looked around, searching for a good reason to explain his panic. *What is going on inside these woods?*

When he heard the flapping of the wings, it was already too late to do anything about it. The moment the talons of the creature penetrated his shoulders the forest echoed with his pained scream.

Dropping his axe, Ornsell could do nothing but bare the excruciating pain of his whole body being carried aloft by some large feathered monstrosity through the gap in the forest. As they rose he grabbed desperately at the clawed talons, but he could barely move his arms the brutal grip was so tight. HThe talons sunk in even deeper and then he passed out. Moments later, Ornsell regained his senses only to find himself released from the grip of the monster and falling on the outskirts of the forest, close to his home. His steep fall was painful, knocking the wind from him. The flapping stopped with a solid thump on the ground next to him.

"It has been years since the last time I saw humans. You haven't changed a bit, still fragile and puny, like maggots swinging their tails to the sun." A woman's twisted voice boomed behind him. Unable to talk, Ornsell tried to keep up by examining the talking creature. "Oh, you're still conscious. That is commendable. You're lucky that I'm not here to kill you, human, although you'll soon wish I had. I'm here to deliver a curse to you and let the world know that we're back. The legends have come back to life, and soon every nightmare will haunt you whilst you still lie awake without slumber."

Ornsell heard the hoarse voice of the monster mumble in a language unknown to him. His eyes were barely able to focus on the monster's figure; hands full of dark feathers, long feet that ended in sharp talons, pitch black eyes. The legends were true when they spoke of dark creatures that once roamed the land of Theugua. This creature was one of the worst, a harpy witch.

Her feathered hands moved in unison, her words giving a hazy rhythm. The dark magic of those creatures needed no instrument or guidance. Sounds coming from the darkest corners of his mind made a crude melody to accompany them. Being a Bard in the past, Ornsell knew something of magic. Whatever magic this creature had done to him seemed bad indeed.

She took a step forward and looked over him. With one of her black feathers, she touched the wound in his back. A drop of scarlet blood glistened on the feather when she stepped away. With a sharp pull, she uprooted it from her body and let the droplet run all the way to its root. When the dark red sparkle dropped to the earth, a feeling like fire started spreading from Ornsell's legs and up his back. Cackling like some insane parrot, the harpy witch swiped him across his cheek with a sharp talon then vaulted into the sky, cackling as she flew away into the distance.

His feverish thoughts ran wild. The burning feeling in his legs and back was getting worse with each passing second. Pain usually sharpened his senses, but the throbbing pain just clouded his mind. *I have to get home. I have to. . . ,* but he was unable to complete that thought. His body was stubborn like most people from Midvein, with a strong mind. Blinded by pain and rage, he thought of his family as he crawled towards his home.

Vygarast chortled as he escorted young Noelene to the mansion just outside of Midvein. He was with a beautiful young girl who was pleasant company for him. Noelene was a sweet servant to the local royalty and was destined to live and die under the command of her mistress. But even though her fate was already known, Noelene always shared her sweetest smile with everyone.

The young Bard knew that he would soon complete his training under master Lanarast (that old geezer was always boozing and piping) and that he would soon venture out of Midvein to see the world. However, Noelene was still a great pleasure to be with. The young woman was quick to complain that she imposed on him, but every time they arrived in front of Vygarast's house, she stopped and insisted they stand together to say their goodbye.

"Don't worry sweet Noelene. My father is a grown man and can stand a few hours without my company."

She blushed as Vygarast approached her and put his hand around her shoulders. "But my mistress always sees us together. I can't let her think that something is happening between us. It would dishonor her and Lady Aderfell. I can't do that to her."

Embarrassed, she lowered her eyes and tried to get away from Vygarast's sweet but firm grip. But the young man was charming and his bright green eyes had long cast their net to catch Noelene's heart. "Don't worry. If that ever happens, I will restore your honor by asking your hand in wedding. You know that I'm an honorable man, one who always keeps his word, right?"

The blond girl did not answer. Her eyes were wide open, her hand stretched, pointing towards Vygarast's house.

"What is going on Noelene? Is everything okay?" Before he was able to complete his thought, Vygarast looked towards the house himself.

He strode as fast as he could, almost losing his footing a couple of times along his way, hurrying to his father's motionless body. He was a bloody mess on the ground and Ornsell growled like a wounded animal when Vygarast got to him.

"Father! Father, what's wrong? Father, who did this to you?"

With great pain and with the last of his immense strength, Ornsell whispered in an agonized voice: "...harpy witch..."

Chapter 2 : Lanarast the Bold

A buzzing tavern full of life was off limits for Lanarast's young pupils. A regular himself, the grizzled man knew the allure of strong liquor and a good patch of tobacco. As a half-elf and prone to the magic flows of the world, Lanarast the Bold was one of the most famed Bards in the Northern Realms. Now, his kingdom was The Hunted Fawn, the one and only tavern of Midvein.

A wooden structure, mostly built to offer cover to a small counter and a busy kitchen, the Fawn was popular for its meat pies and the always-lively company of the veteran warriors.

"That old man Ornsell is late again. I hate to start all by myself."

Lanarast was seated on a wooden stool next to the counter, waiting for his friend to arrive. Having an early drink was just plain misery if you did not have company to share it with. That's what Ornsell used to say. He was also the one with family in the Mainland where the world was more active and lords fought over broken hearts and old grievances. The letters his wife sent him were a treasure for Ornsell and Lanarast both, two people who were once great travelers of Theugua.

With a generous swill from his glass, Lanarast promised to get back on the training grounds if Ornsell was not there by the time he emptied his drink. *He's always a fool for punctuality and now he's late like a bride on her wedding day.*

He checked the only other company that had sought refuge in a mug of ale so early in the day. Three hunters, all of them heavily dressed, shivering under the North's cold touch. Winters north of Theugua were harsh. Everybody knew that. For three seasoned hunters to shiver like that there was only one possible explanation.

Mirthful as he was from consuming alcohol, Lanarast grabbed his glass of mulled wine and headed towards the three men. As soon as they saw him stride straight towards them, the two men standing at the end of a tall table lowered their hands to touch the hilts of their short axes. *Now that's an interesting reaction. Men of the king, I'm certain, strangers to these parts.*

"I wouldn't advice you to start a fight in here, sirs. Rhene will throw you out and me as well and I would be banned from coming back in for a week. And that would be a long week indeed. I'm here to learn news from the Mainland."

The men took quick glances at each other, trying to weigh the situation. A direct approach was dangerous, Lanarast knew that more than anyone did, but he was getting impatient, and he had promised himself not to indulge in a second glass of wine before noon. Slowly the two men drew their hands away from their swords and nodded for Lanarast to join them.

"Thank you." Lanarast said in a cheerful voice. "So tell me, what are the King's men doing so far North? I thought that the four Dukes were on bad terms with the King."

The red-headed man of the three, with a weak jaw and sharp cheekbones snapped first. "Our business is not ours to discuss with a sot like you. His Majesty Gabriel the Second, the Honored Seat of Rolis, is the only rightful ruler of Theugua. You better remember that. "

Okay, that was intense. There is certainly something going on here. Of the three men, the one sitting on Lanarast's right was silently examining him. A black-haired man with broad shoulders and who seemed like he was trying hard to hold his tongue. All the same, his eyes suddenly sparked in recognition. *Oh boy. Here we go.*

"Excuse me sir. I think he's one of the Great Bards of Duke Hyntorn, the Southern Overseer." As the words left the young man's mouth, Lanarast looked up in disdain.

The young officer was suddenly feeling less confident of his authority. "I... well... excuse me sir. I didn't know."

"You didn't know because there was no reason for you to. I'm retired now, living my life peacefully. Nevertheless, I won't take up any more of your time. Your presence alone is bad news enough for this village." As Lanarast turned and headed for the door, he couldn't help but overhear a muffled round of grunts coming from each one of them.

His lips twisted into a foxy grin. *My days as Lanarast the Bold are long past. Nowadays my only act of courage is to return home late in the evening with my breath smelling of booze.* Lanarast laughed, thinking of the reaction his wife took every time something like that happened.

He was standing next to the door when a sudden push on the door almost hit him in the face. "What in the... ? Vygarast? How many times have I told you...?" Before he was able to to scold his young pupil, the boy had muttered many times the same sentence, drawing the man's attention.

"My dad has been attacked by a harpy."

Vygarast had a hard time staying put and not running for his house as fast as he was able. As his master, Lanarast the Bold held him up and forced him to tell the whole story. The young man was no longer so sure he should have come after him. *Maybe I should have gone straight to the healer.*

"Let me get this straight," he repeated, "your father was attacked by a harpy? A real harpy? Like the harpy witches of the myth?"

Vygarast quieted as he started to recite the whole story again. "I was walking Noelene to the mansion when I saw my father on the ground just outside our home. When I got to his side, he said "witch harpy" and then would ramble on incoherently about the witch cursing him and harpies in the sky. His back has two great injuries, like a wild animal had attacked him. By the time I took him inside our house, he had passed out and was barely breathing."

The young man saw deep lines forming on Vygarast's forehead. He was troubled, and for the first time in Vygarast's life, he looked his age. "You can't tell anyone about this... alright? Not Noelene, not your friends, not anyone! Harpies are creatures of myth, monsters that have the power to use magic without instruments. Even for us half-elves, that is not an easy task. Now quickly, bring me to your father!"

They could see Vygarast's house in the distance as they quickly jogged to it. Noelene was outside, standing close to the door, waiting for them. Vygarast fell deep into his thoughts, running his hand through his black hair and trying to make sense of his master's words. "So, is it true? My father was cursed by a witch harpy of myth? But. . .how? Why? I mean, I knew my father was also a Bard for a couple years, but he's not so gifted in magic as we are. I don't understand why a harpy would attack him."

"Neither do I, Vygarast." Lanarast replied calmly. For now we have to find out if your father is indeed cursed." Lanarast pulled his flute from his overcoat.

Vygarast was curious now, trying to figure out why his master brought out his flute. "Is there a song that could cure him? Or let us know if he had been touched by dark magic?"

Even though they were in a great hurry, Lanarast stopped what he was doing and glared at young Vygarast with his piercing green eyes. "There is no dark, or light magic son. Magic is a unity, a great flow of things that exist. If you use the same spell to help, or do harm, then the dark one is you, not your magic. Remember that... it may save your life one day."

Vygarast took a step back, startled by his master serious note. He had never seen him so concerned, not once in his whole life. "I'm sorry master. You're right. It was my fault. But how can a curse be the same as a song that we cast? I still don't get it."

Lanarast returned to his long strides, and Vygarast was the one now trying to keep up. "A curse usually takes something out of the caster's body, and infuses it with something from the victim's. For example, I could use my blood to cast a spell of healing on you, and I could also add a lock of your hair, then the same spell modified a bit could suddenly harm you. It's a complicated process, one that no one should have to know, not me, not you, not anyone. But during war, there were many times that I was called to lift curses from other Bards."

Just a couple strides away from their house, Vygarast was suddenly hit by renewed hope. "So that means you can lift it, right?"

"We'll see son, we'll see."

As they arrived at the house, Noelene had a shocked expression on her face. Vygarast urged his master to go inside so he could talk to his friend. "What is going on Vygarast? Why did you call for master Lanarast and not the healer?" asked Noelene with a concerned expression on her face.

He combed her hair with his hand, trying to calm her down. "Lanarast is a veteran of many wars and my father always warned me when I was younger that if there was ever a problem then to contact Lanarast immediately. I'm not sure what is going on, but it would be better if you left."

Noelene grabbed Vygarast's smooth hand and intertwined her fingers with his. "I think someone cursed him Vygarast," she said with her voice lowered so that master Lanarast could not hear. "He kept gibbering on about harpies and witches while you were gone. I think someone used dark magic on him." She said shivering.

She then leaned in to kiss him quickly, wished him good luck, then she left, never turning her head back even for a moment. *What if she's right, what if someone cast a terrible curse on him?*

He took a deep breath and stepped inside the house. His master had already started singing *The Long Tale of Etna and River*; a healing spell that was said to be able to remove any traces of malicious magic. It was called long for a reason and as Vygarast walked in; his master was just completing the first verse.

It was a difficult spell, one that needed the utmost focus, steep changes to the musical rhythm, and even some vocal parts that only the best of Bards could sing. Lanarast was one of the best, that was true, but his version was a bit choppy and at some points even discordant.

Vygarast wanted to tell him that he was doing it wrong, but who was he to challenge a legend among the Bards? It was easily half an hour later that they started seeing results to the singing. During that time, Vygarast had contemplated every possible outcome of this casting. He knew that this song was strong and he hoped that it would not be enough.

Magic cast with instruments is ten times stronger than regular magic. It was like the wooden flute was putting the flows of magic through a prism. That way, instead of making one strong, dangerous flow, it was able to drain only a thread of it at a time, making it less dangerous. *At least, that was what his master had told him. But creatures of the past did not use instruments in their magic. If that was true. . .*

A flash of light blinded both the men inside the room. The song was suddenly over, and Ornsell was still lying on his bed, unable to move. However, his wounds had been healed and there was no apparent reason why he still couldn't move.

"Damn it!" Lanarast said suddenly after several minutes of waiting. "This is not good boy. Your father is cursed by a creature of myth. There is no Bard in the whole kingdom that can lift his curse, not without casting solely with his hands. And for that to work, someone would have to recite the whole *Etna and River* bare, meaning sure death, or at the very least madness before the song would even be completed. This is bad, son, really bad."

Vygarast could not help but think of all those nights that he and his father used to spend alone. His mother, an elf of the woods, did not age like humans and as a half-elf himself, he would be blessed with a long life if he was lucky. Eventually his mother left, unable to bear the sight of his father as he aged and leaving the two of them alone to survive out in Midvein.

He couldn't, he wouldn't forgive himself if his father died from magic, the same magic he wanted to use to become a legend like his master. Vygarast felt the burdens of regret weighing on his shoulder. He was always out, having fun with his friends. It was his fault that his father was cursed. He knew that somehow, he could have helped him if he was out there with him like he was supposed to be that day.

"Step outside master. If there is someone that should get hurt to lift that curse, that should be me." Instead of Lanarast scolding him, the man started laughing, getting on young Vygarast's nerves. "Have you gone mad as well master?"

He stood up and rested his hand on Vygarast's shoulder. He put on a serious expression but there was a twinkle in his eyes. "There is still hope. Tell me, Vygarast, do you know the legend of the Owl Wizard?"

Chapter 3 : The Jewel of the North

Vygarast was standing on a hilltop, two spans away from a town named Crowfair. He could hear the commotion coming from the outer side of the walls as clearly as if he was standing next to it.

Probably an early Spring festival is on the way, or traders flocking in front of the gates, Vygarast thought as he took a long glance ahead of him before starting for the town. Either way, it was not his business to care about festivals right now as was made perfectly clear by his appearance.

Wearing a heavy, dark cloak with the hood on, his face was covered so as to pass unseen by the guards. It was Lanarast's idea to travel lightly and stealthily. Vygarast couldn't help but feel indebted to his master after everything he had done to help him. The whole plan to chase after a legend was Lanarast's, and it was also Vygarast's only hope of saving his father.

A couple days before, both Vygarast and his master were standing above Ornsell's paralyzed body. Vygarast was ready to start singing the tale of Etna and River using only his voice, when his master stopped him to tell him an old story that he knew all too well.

"The Greedy Owl-Wizard? The one who would make any wish come true for 1000 gold coins? Wasn't that supposed to be a fairytale?" Vygarast had told his master then, his hands outstretched and ready to raise his voice.

"As you can see my boy, legends may have started walking on these grounds again. If you want to save your father, then this might be our only hope. "

The deep-lined former hero took his place next to the hearth, in the rocking chair that Vygarast's father used to sway for endless hours in. For some reason, the young man felt like a child once again, when he was always bothering his father to tell him another story, grinning next to him by the hearth. The one with the greedy, long-bearded wizard, who asked for golden coins to lift curses, was one of his favorites.

"I know the tale by heart, master."

"Could you recite it for me?" Lanarast said, glaring straight at the hearth with empty eyes.

"Yes, of course." Vygarast hummed before starting. "Deep in the forest of Streyln, there was a creature of old. A man and an animal both, with eyes wide like an owl, with a nose hooked and pointy. The Owl-Wizard he was called, and he would make any wish come true for gold. A thousand and one was his price, in coins or gems that would sparkle."

"That's enough. Thank you, son. So, do you get it now? If you want to help your father, then you better start with coming up with one thousand and one gold coins first, and then head south to Crowfair in the Streyln woods. It won't be an easy task, certainly not for a Bard still in training. However, it is our only hope, and I would advise you to follow it. I will tend to your father as much as I can while you're away, but as he is now, he does not have too long before the dark magic of the curse crushes his soul. I am the only one who will be able to keep him alive and give you enough time to return."

Vygarast thought about it for a minute, trying to figure out if searching for an old legend was the best solution to his problem. Of course, casting a spell with bare hands was not a good idea, a foolish one in fact. But going after the legend of some greedy owl wizard could be the end of his father's life, and his, if he was not careful.

"Master Lanarast, tell me. Do you honestly believe that monsters of legend are back in this world?"

Lanrast swung back and forth in the old, wooden rocking chair, creaking the floor boards underneath. He took his time to answer. "I don't know for sure. There are only tales and fragments of books about the ages of old. Everything we know, we've learned from traditions and customs. I don't believe there is another good reason that we still leave our leftovers outside our houses for luck if that hasn't something to do with those creatures of the old. However, the Owl-Wizard's tale is very detailed (too detailed I'd say) to have been spawn from one man's vivid imagination."

"But I can't go away chasing shadows master. Maybe if we try together. . ."

"Listen Vygarast, your father will die if you don't trust me. I can sustain him with my magic while you are gone, otherwise he will perish quickly. Here, take my flute and lute. They should help you and I have some spares. But you need to go. Time is of the essence. Go to Crowfair and search for signs of other creatures there. Crowfair is a bigger town than Midvein, one that traders pass through all the time. If there is a place where you would hear about old legends or chances for gold, then Crowfair is our best bet."

Vygarast thought about it for a moment. There was no harm in taking a short trip to Crowfair, not when his master had promised to take care of his father until he returned. Lanarast was right. Everybody on the North side of the Stryqip Bluff knew that rumors and good gold only come from Crowfair in these parts. At least that was what his father had always told to him. If he had a chance of finding something out about monsters and magic, Crowfair was the place.

The young pupil lowered his head in respect and grabbed his master's instruments from the table. They then talked a bit more about the hardships of the trip, with the path between the two towns still covered in part with heavy snow. Vygarast had taken the trip with his father many times in the past, so he knew the path well enough to travel. They finalized the plans and then Vygarast waited for his master to sing one last song of healing before he left for his home to gather some supplies. As Lanarast left, Vygarast went to sit by his father.

His father was unnaturally still all night, frightening him. *What has befallen you father? I swear, I'll find who did this to you and make them pay.* He thought as he got up from beside his father's bed.

Vygarast spent the rest of the night and the next morning getting ready until Lanarast arrived with a heavy bag of supplies. Some of them were resources for Vygarast, while others were clothes for himself. He was planning to spend his nights here until Vygarast returned. They exchanged some words for good luck and then Lanarast gave him a giant hug.

Vygarast then kissed his father on the cheek, praying that it wouldn't be the last time he saw him alive. As Vygarast left his home, his heart raged with anger that steeled his will. *I'll be back with a cure and that witches head, father.*

Two days of long walks in the frozen edges of the Howling Pass took Vygarast outside Crowfair's tall walls. Unlike Midvein, on the other side of the Stryqip Bluff (which was mostly called that as a jest to the Southerners who dared travel so far up north), Crowfair was a popular destination for merchants and travelers alike.

'Those who control the Crow's Jewel, also control the far sides of the North.' Everyone used to say that back in Midvein, but after seeing Crowfair now for the first time in five long years, Vygarast was not so sure anyone could call the town a Jewel anymore, not unless they meant the cheap ones.

Getting closer to the town, Vygarast could see many pairs of plump loafers that called themselves guards roam the outer side of the walls. Their laughter could be heard loud and clear even to Vygarast's ears, who was still a good ways from the main gate. He turned his head in disdain, trying to avoid eye contact with all those worthless souls, as the guards where known to be vicious and thoroughly corrupt. Unfortunately, Crowfair was also known for another reason, for mischievous men and sly women.

"Hey, you, you with the black hood, don't act like you can't hear me!" A hoarse voice, one belonging to one of those swine on guard duty, forced him to stop. Vygarast raised his head just an inch, aiming to intimidate the man and at the same time get an eye on the boor that couldn't even trouble himself from putting down his meal. He was holding a piece of pork's loin in his right hand, and in his other hand was a half-empty glass of dark red wine.

"Excuse me, guard. Is something wrong?" Vygarast's voice was sweet and rich. His bright green eyes sparkled as if tiny rays of sunlight fell upon them, the effect enhanced by the raised hood. His green eyes were always a cause of admiration everywhere he went. Likewise, the guard was drawn to their color for a moment before taking a large bite from his pork loin.

Vygarast was a good-looking young man, but certainly not one cut out for fistfights. The guard seemed to understand that all too well, so his brute behavior was magnified by his sense of superiority. Vygarast, however, was an apprentice Bard, and a good one as well. There were reasons his master asked him to travel incognito. Avoiding the King's men was not the only one.

"If you follow my orders" the guard said with a mouthful of food, "then we won't have a problem. His Highness, Lord Digby the First, would feel greatly appreciated if word got to his ears that guests honored," he put a great emphasis on that word, "the hard-working guards of Crowfair, the North's Jewel, with a pair of gold coins."

The man's sly smile said more than the man intended. This was a polite way, if it could be called anything like that coming from that brood's mouth, of asking him for a bribe them to let him in without trouble. People like that disgusted Vygarast, so he decided to give the man a good lesson.

"I'm sorry sir, I didn't know that Lord Digby himself was so closely affiliated to his gate guards. Unfortunately, I've just returned from the mines and I'm with empty pockets. Could I reward you instead with an appetizing song, one that would help you enjoy your meal even more?"

The man looked the other members of his bunch only to see them nod excitedly. A good entertainer was a rare occasion in the slums outside the city. A performance, if good enough, was as valuable as a few pieces of gold to some. He knew that if he said no, then it would be like returning a very expensive gift for no good reason.

"Suit yourself. But, tell us one of those long ones. My boys deserve the best," he said and a loud cheer echoed from everywhere around the gate.

Vygarast set down his pouch with a silent thump and dug out his master's flute. He examined it with a thoughtful look and nodded to himself. *This will be enough for them.* He mentally counted the men close to him, and with a measured move, he touched the hilt of his sword from inside his cloak. A small crowd had now amassed around them, getting ready for the show. When Vygarast was ready to start, he took a long breath in and started talking out loud:

"Ladies and esteemed men of Crowfair! The tale I'll sing to you is one of passion, courage, and heroism. Remember it, learn from it, and in the future, don't use your lord's name to gain from it." The guards had barely enough time to move before Vygarast started his song.

It was that of a Nymph of the High Peaks, the frozen slopes of the Oversea Mountains. The song was used as a way to freeze up the Bard's enemies, inflicting them with a spell that immobilized their every move. By the time the Bard had started his song, the men had slowed down considerably, now almost unable to move at all.

Vygarast knew all too well that the only throwback of his spell was that it was easily broken if he moved. His plan, however, was not to freeze them completely; the spell had also another use. "Now, let's see how strong and mighty you are," he sang.

The men were now able to move again, but their shaky limbs deemed them unable to fight. They drew their swords with great difficulty and as they launched forward to meet the Bard, Vygarast outmaneuvered them with ease, succeeding in tripping a couple of them so that they fell on their arses. The crowd was now laughing at the guards' misfortune and clapped every time a freezing guard fell on his face.

Once all the guards where left unable to move on the ground, Vygarast curtsied and the crowd cheered. "Thank you, thank you good men and women of Crowfair. If you could point me at a good inn for the night, then…" Before he was able to complete his sentence, a guard from inside the walls hurdled towards him with an angry roar.

Usually, Bards were not trained in the act of fighting because they were mostly used as healers or to keep the soldiers' morale high. However, Vygarast was Lanarast's pupil, and he didn't get the name Lanarast the Bold from just his skill with magic alone. His master had insisted that all his students be trained, like he was, in the art of swordsmanship.

'There is no greater danger than a slow Bard, or an untrained one. You can learn to sing, but for a Bard to cast he needs absolute focus. You won't always have the time to sing, not during a fight."

Abruptly, with a quick flap of his cloak, Vygarast drew his sword. When the two steel blades kissed, the crowd gasped in delight. In their minds, this was closer to a show than an actual fight. Vygarast was quick, sleek, always a move ahead of his enemy. His sword was like an extension to his body, and he moved with practiced grace.

The young blue-eyed guard was soon exhausted, and fell to his knees when Vygarast disarmed him with a well-placed blow. The crowd cheered and Vygarast turned and bowed a few times quickly to thank them. He was, above all, a showman.

For a reason apparent to all, the remaining guards avoided him, instead tending to their officer and their fallen comrades as Vygarast swiftly made his way into the city. A few in the crowd followed him, cheering his performance. After several blocks a gray-haired old man called out to Vygarast. His face was a mixture of concern and caution. He instinctively knew that the elder wanted to ask him something.

"Sir... Sir Bard," the man stuttered and lowered his head in respect, "I'm Elder Vint, chief of one of the villages near the forest of Streyln. Sir Bard, I have been looking for a hero such as you for many days. I wouldn't ask for such a tedious act if I could avoid it, but do you know anything about killing Ogres?"

Chapter 4 : Of Spiders and Fairies

Elder Vint was certainly quick on his feet for an old man. Hunching forward, sometimes even skipping a step while keeping up a fast pace. He looked like he was being chased by a pack of wild dogs.

Trotting now and then to keep up with the man's fast walking, Vygarast was having second thoughts of following the man towards the woods. However, just the mention of Ogres, gigantic super strong beasts with fierce tempers, was enough of a hook for young Vygarast to help.

There is no way of him knowing that I'm out to hunt legends, right? I mean, I kept my face hidden all the way from Midvein to Crowfair, as well as kept my business secret. Vygarast took a long breath and decided it was time to ask this old man some questions.

"Excuse me, Vint, can we make a short stop? The fight and casting exhausted me and I would like to have a word with you now that we're some ways away from the city."

The elder argued with himself for a short moment, probably weighing his options in his head. The man wanted a fighter and Vygarast, even with then prowess he showed, would not be able to kill an Ogre if he was tired. So, with a sharp nod, he led the way deeper into the woods, this time at a more manageable pace.

A couple spans to the west there was a small glade. Judging from the blackened ground in the middle surrounded by stones, this was a hunters' spot. The elder certainly knew his way around. Vygarast's had a big concern. For some time now, he had a vile taste in his mouth, like the air tasted bad. He had asked the elder about it, but he didn't seem to notice.

As they stopped to rest Vygarast stated: "Thank you elder. Some times people tend to forget that magic comes equal parts from inside and from outside the body. No matter how powerful a Bard is, casting takes a lot from a man." Vygarast knew that this was not totally true, but if he was getting lured into a trap, then lying to a freckled old man was the least of his worries.

"I understand young Bard. Rest for a while. But we do have to be in the village by sundown." Vygarast noticed a tint of concern on the man's voice. *It seems that forests are not safe anymore.*

"Tell me elder. What do you know of the Ogre?" The old man snapped at the sound of that word, acting like he heard of the creature from the first time ever in his life.

"Not much. Mostly rumors, glimpses of shadows deep into the Streyln. But just recently, a bunch of our best hunters decided to hunt that. . .thing. No one believed that it was an Ogre, not with the hundreds of years that we hadn't seen one of those things in our forests. Only after one of the hunters returned, with blood running from his amputated arm, did we know for sure. The last word he muttered was 'Ogre' before he died from blood loss. I couldn't wait any longer for someone to believe me. I had to act, so I decided to get to Crowfair and ask for help. But Lord Digby laughed at me, believing me to be a frightened old man who was daft in the head."

Yes, that is something that a Crowfairer would do, Vygarast thought. "And tell me elder, is there a bounty on the beast's head?"

A bold question, Vygarast knew, but he needed gold! Besides, everyone knows that beast slaying was not a free job. Lanarast was rich in his old age from all the bounties he had collected. "Yes, of course young Bard, we managed to collect 50 gold coins; it was a rough winter for our village, and we were unable to gather more."

Damn. Not even a fraction of what I want. I should have asked about the money first. But Vygarast knew that he followed the man because he needed to be bold and he wanted to be sure of himself before going to look for the Owl-Wizard. It was one thing hearing his own father talk about harpies, but for a whole village to believe in Ogres was huge. He had to investigate. "Okay. I'll do my best to help you Elder Vint."

Half an hour had passed while the two men talked to each other. The Elder's village, Hollowpeak, was mostly a settlement used by passing hunters. Deep in the forest and close to the river of Turtle Run, Hollowpeak was a village of few permanent residents but with plenty of visitors coming and going from Crowfair. The fact that the army, or even other hunters, had not taken notice of the Ogre was something that worried Vygarast. It was too late now, since he had already committed to the task and followed the man to the other side of the forest. He could only to hope for the best.

After taking a last sip off his flask, Vygarast was ready at last to move on from the forest clearing. He was still uncertain of the elder's intentions, but at least he had had time to replenish his strength. Magic could do wonders to his stamina, but it could also leave a man hollow if used carelessly. The old man obviously didn't know that a Bard could use magic to prolong his stamina or run faster, but Vygarast had no intention of being careless and running head-first into a trap. His father's life depended on him.

"Okay, let's go. Is Hollowpeak still far?" He asked, turning to look for the old man behind him. When Vygarast finally spotted him, the elder was shaking like a fish out of the water. It was like he had seen a ghost.

"Is something wrong?" As Vygarast rushed back to help him, he saw what scared the man senseless. "What the. . . ?" He didn't have time to speak.

He pushed the elder roughly one way and then jumped himself the other way, just in time to dodge a huge spider attacking him from above. Having lived most of his life at the foot of a mountain close to the forest, Vygarast had only seen a few giant snakes the size of this thing. Its hairy belly hit the forest floor and it waved its front legs in front of vicious mouth dripping with poison. It was getting ready to attack.

"Run! I will keep it here," Vygarast bellowed to the old man who stood petrified a few feet away. "Run you stupid old man! I'll catch up with you!" After the second round of shouts, Elder Vint shook his head and ran into the woods.

Now, focus on the spider Vygarast. He drew his sword from the scabbard and held it with both his hands for more power. Sharp as his blade was, Vygarast knew he had to end this fight with a mighty blow if he wanted to survive. The spider's fangs dripped green venom and as it prepared to attack.

Vygarat examined his surroundings, searching for the best footing. *If only master Lanarast was here. He could cast while I slaughtered it with ease.* But he knew he was alone in this. Vygarast took a deep breath, relaxed his muscles and followed his gut.

Hello? Is anyone out there?

"What the? Who was that?" Everything then happened almost simultaneously. The enormous spider jumped towards Vygarast who had lost his concentration when the voice had whispered inside his head. It was the chirpy sound of a female voice. Vygarast could not track to its source. Lost in the moment, he barely managed to jump to the side, barely avoiding the spider's fangs. The spider responded quickly and did a quick jump turn, and started charging after Vygarast.

He didn't have the time to think. He took his sword and thrust if forward, catching the spider between its many eyes. The hairy creature was fast, however, and managed to get away with his blade only sinking in a few inches deep. Quickly circling, getting behind Vygarast's back, the spider attacked again. Spinning with the sword above his head, Vygarast brought his sword down in a might two handed cleave that tore through the spiders head and brain. With a horrifying shriek, the spider fell to the ground with its belly up and its legs twitching. Vygarast wasted no time and gave the beast a few more deadly stabs until the twitching finally stopped.

Gasping for breath while standing above the spider, Vygarast shakily cleaned his sword on his nearby tall grass. He was exhausted.

Excuse me, now that the battle is over, can you help me here?

"Damn it, who's there?" Vygarast shouted, almost jumping out of his skin when the voice whispered inside his mind again. "Are you one of those creatures? What do you want?" Exhausted and unsure of himself, Vygarast peered all around the forest.

Hey... human, I'm over here. Turn around.

He turned his head, trying to locate the voice. "I can't see you!" Abruptly, a small, flickering motion of light appeared on a glistening spider's web between the trunks of two trees. Vygarast rubbed his eyes and blinked a few times before being sure. Something was indeed on that web and it certainly was not a fly.

Vygarast held his sword ready as he made his way to the silky web and the small glowing bundle that was trapped within. The voice was silent now, probably eager to be set free. His hands shook as he stretched them out to rip the webs strands apart. It took him a minute or two to completely remove the bundle from the powerful and sticky spider web.

A big web for a big spider, thought Vygarast as he examined the glowing ball.

I agree. I really hate spiders! The voice replied to his thoughts, making Vygarast jump and look around with wild eyes.

"Okay, the fun is over. What kind of spell is that? And how can you cast without an instrument? I haven't heard a song or anything." He took a good, long look around, waiting for someone to appear and assure him that everything was a joke, however, only that small light appeared out the mass of spider web.

Listen you hasty, young human; my name is Azore Frostyhill, and I'm of the Fairy Daughters. I would be delighted if you stopped your nonsense and freed me from the rest of this web.

Vygarast delicately pulled the glob of web apart, revealing a small glowing fairy from within. She squealed and cursed as he tried his best to delicately remove her from the rest of the sticky mess. He took out his water skin and after a few more minutes of careful work, she was free. She smiled at him then and then waved her hands about in a mysterious gesture. She glowed as bright as the sun for a brief second and then she was flying in the air next to his head.

Now that she was so close to him, Vygarast could see her for what she really was, another legend; a woman, or a teenage girl, with long blonder hair that changed color towards the end. Her eyes were two tiny balls of fire, like the flare that remained for a few seconds after you blew out a candle. Her body was tiny and her wings like that of a beautiful butterfly.

She looked tired, so Vygarast said: "Here, you can rest on my shoulder." With a quirky sound, the fairy landed on the edge of his right shoulder. The feeling of having her there was invigorating; it was like her very presence filled Vygarast with strength and power.

Now what? Aren't you going to tell me your name? The melodic voice chimed in his head.

"Oh, yes. I'm sorry. We half-elves don't meet fairies all that commonly around here." Vygarast grinned in an effort to appease the small creature. "I'm Vygarast son of Ornsell, from Midvein of the North Side of the Stryqip Bluff." The fairy smiled.

Pretty big name for such a young human. Are you a lord, or royalty? I really love palace gardens. Vygarast could almost sense her weary smile.

"Unfortunately, I'm not... Lady Frostyhill. I'm on a quest to save my father from a harpy's curse. I was following an old man to his village to kill an ogre, when we met the spider. You know what happened after that."

As soon as everything poured out of his mouth, Vygarast cupped his mouth with both his hands, every secret he meant to keep, out in the light. The tiny fairy giggled at his reaction. *You ignorant human; you really don't know anything about our kind, do you?* With a brief flap of her beautiful wings, the fairy proceeded to explain. *No one can lie around fairies, not even Bards. We are nature's judges and protectors, keeping our Mother safe from every vile creature, especially humans.*

The tiny fairy floated before Vygarast's head, looking him straight in the eyes. For a moment, she examined him. *You have unusually bright green eyes, even for a human.*

"I'm a half-elf, which has something to do with it."

A charming giggle erupted from the fairy, this time lighting the whole glade up. *My dear Vygarast, I wish I could stay. However, you have to take me to your King now, or one of your Lords. I bear news from the Queen of Fairies herself, and it is urgent.*

Chapter 5 : The Four Dukes of Theugua

Vygarast returned to his camp from his short visit to the village. He had spent the last night talking with Azore, or Azy as she preferred to be called, who was a fairy ambassador sent here to negotiate the return of fairies to the kingdom. Azore Frostyhill was a Winter Fairy, belonging to one of the Four Factions of hierarchy back in the Fairy Kingdom.

She wouldn't reveal too much to him, not with her diplomatic mission under way, but she and Vygarast became friends quite fast. Being forced to say the truth while close to her was troubling at first, but soon it was refreshing to not have to keep anything hidden from her. Even so, Azy was a quirky fairy, even under fairy standards. She was really talkative, not easy to fool (Vygarast was pretty sure that this was a common characteristic between the fairies) and a restless spirit overall. She was good company to have and Vygarast enjoyed every second.

It was not easy for Vygarast to accept that he was now friends with a creature from lore, but he was loving his new friend. He pulled aside a bush to enter his camp after searching for the old man for several hours. Azy was hiding on the higher branches of a tree and she floated down to greet him. It was very cool that she didn't have to flap her wings in order to fly. He wasn't sure how she did that.

So? What happened? Did you find the old man? Now that she had rested for a whole night, she flew up and down cheerfully, showing her emotions in a pretty vivid way.

"Vint managed to return safely in his village. The only thing I was able to extract from him was that the hunters had tracked the Ogre's location to the south side of the Streyln forest, close to. . ."

The wizard's tower, she interrupted, *this is wrong. A wizard would never let an Ogre so close to his tower, not without blasting it to bits. Something is wrong here, Vygarast. Maybe we should go visit the king.*

"No. I'm sorry Lady Azy, but. . ."

I told you before, I'm not a Lady. I'm just a messenger.

"Yes, yes. Sorry. But you have to trust me on this. The king will not help us, not without some kind of personal interest involved. Elder Vint asked for aid, and was thrown out with empty hands. Also my father. . ."

Yes, you're right. It's just that.. well, fairies and wizards are like opposites. We are Nature's gentle side, while wizards are rough and dangerous with their powers. You don't want to have anything to do with a wizard, unless your life is in danger.

"I need to save my father... even if I die in the attempt" Vygarast said seriously. He lowered his hood to reveal his tattooed face to Azy. She gasped, as if seeing it for the first time; maybe she did see it for the first time. The little fairy was so shaken from her adventure last night that she had fallen asleep almost immediately.

What is that on your face? Did they hurt you back there? She flew closer to his face, examining the inked shape. It was still small, just five years in the making, covering the better part of his face and just starting to expand to his shoulder blade.

"Oh, that? Well, this is a half-elf thing. Didn't half-elves in the past have tattoos on their faces?"

Elves, as I knew them, would never mate with a human. Creatures that aren't touched by time like us see the fleeting life of the humans as an abomination, a curse from our Mother. So, afraid of losing their immortality, elves would never even think about sleeping with humans.

"Well, things have changed nowadays. Half-elves are as common as humans. We don't share immortality with our magical half, but we live longer than humans do and we have the same passions. Contrary to our elven brothers, we celebrate life and death, getting magical tattoos on our body. The longer the tattoo on the day of your death, the fuller you life was. It is something every half-elf does when they come of age. I've never given it much thought."

The fairy touched the tattoo and then jumped off his shoulder quickly. Vygarast could sense her quizzical face. His voice stopped her in her tracks. He had more news to share. "Azy, your quest might turn up being more difficult than mine. Back in the village, I saw soldiers of the king ransacking the local shops. I also heard news of the King being on his dying bed. If that is true, the Four Dukes will not stand still until one of them gets his throne."

I don't understand. What has that got to do with my quest?

"It might be years before a new King rises between the Four Dukes, years that would tarnish diplomatic relations unless agreed upon by each Duke separately."

The little fairy gasped in shock, startling Vygarast. Talking to his mind made every interaction between them ten times more intense. When she felt fear, he felt every ripple of her shaken mind, and when she ways happy, euphoria filled him as well. He needed to ask her to tone down her sentiments a bit, but that was not the problem here. Azy had to decide if she would follow Vygarast on his quest to save his father, or start her journey to every side of the kingdom to talk with the Four Dukes.

I know what you're thinking Vygarast, but I can't leave you alone. Surprised, Vygarast started to protest only for Azy to stop him. *You know nothing of our world Vygarast and I know nothing of yours. I was thinking of asking you sooner or later, but now is as good a time as any. Would you like to partner up with me until we complete our quests?*

The young Bard didn't know what to say, or in the current situation, what to think. Bards were meant to travel around and search for new songs, or even write them if talented enough. Before now, Vygarast had never even thought of leaving his father behind, not when his mother and sisters were in the Mainland leaving with the other elves.

But meeting the Four Dukes, learning more about the old legends, and taking part in one of the grandest adventures of his life, surely was an offer he couldn't pass up. On the other hand, Vygarast had responsibilities.

When he opened his mouth to ask for a little time to think about it, he was compelled instead to tell the truth: "Yes! Yes, I would gladly go with you!"

Truth cannot be hidden young human. Remember that at all times.

After picking up his things from the ground and making sure he covered the campfire with enough dirt to bury the coals, he started looking for the Ogre's lair. According to the villagers, after passing the Rose Brook on the south, and getting through the dark part of the forest, there was a clearing near the end of the forest, just steps before meeting the steep wall of a mountain.

It was not a long trip, not for an experienced hunter, or someone familiar with the place, but for two strangers to this land it was a difficult path. Following directions was something that Vygarast had never wrapped his head around. He was constantly getting lost in the mines back home or in the forest near his house. So he took his time and did his best to tread carefully. He didn't want to stumble into a dangerous situation unaware.

They walked, and walked, until the sound of gurgling water revived their hopes. "This must be the river. We are getting closer."

For the greater part of their walk, Azy was flying up and down, exploring the surroundings and asking questions about humans. Abruptly, she decided to rest on Vygarast's shoulder. *Be careful Vygarast. From here on out, danger lurks in every corner.*

They traveled onwards for another thirty minutes. The deep part of the forest was void of sunlight, making Vygarast lower his hood. The tattoo on his face sparkled as tiny rays of sunlight fell upon it. He wasn't exactly sure what came first, the realization that something had caught his left foot, or the pain of a bite higher up on his leg, but Vygarast found himself lying on the wet bank of the rumbling river.

A silent growl, one that couldn't start describing his pain, came from Vygarast's deepest thoughts. It was a growl of fear, realizing he was about to die. The shrieking voice of a teenage girl in his mind quickly made him come to his senses.

Vygarast! Vygarast, stand on your feet! A Hydra has attacked you!

Between the burning sensation of his wounds, the running water dousing his head, and Azy's powerful mental urgings, Vygarast found the strength he needed to jerk violently backwards and then quickly stand on his feet. Blood coursed from his leg as he took a look at the monstrosity before him. The creature before him was like a nightmare come to life, a double-headed snake monster with the feet of a giant lizard.

Without time to pull either of his instruments from his bag, which now lay nearby, Vygarast instinctively grabbed the hilt of his sword and pulled it quickly, going immediately into a defensive stance.

Azy landed on his shoulder and put her small hands on his face. A warm sensation rushed through every vein of his body, leading down to his bleeding leg and aching ankle. In what seemed like seconds, Vygarast's pain faded into a barely-aware numbness. "What did you do?" he wanted to ask but was interrupted by the echoing hiss of the two-headed snake.

Vygarast thought of diving into the river, as he was a powerful swimmer, but his father had taught him that snakes and water was not a good combination. He rolled away from the river bank and towards a dry space further into the dark part of the forest. Until now, he hadn't examined the size of the crawling beast. Vygarast realized that like the spider before, the snake was huge as well, easily four hundred pounds and seven feet tall. The beast charged him suddenly and Vygarast was barely able to do a backwards sidestep just out of reach of the snakes massive fangs. He recovered quickly though, planting his back foot then coming down with a massive two handed over hand chop that sent the nearest head to him rolling away on the ground.

That is not enough. You have to cut both its heads at the same time or else the other will grow back again. Azy didn't have to explain it to him, but the reminder was helpful. Vygarast had heard stories of hydras before and knew of their regenerative powers. The hydra retreated as a big bulk of pink skin started growing to suddenly reveal a new head.

"Damn it. This is not good." Vygarast said to Azy.

But this was his chance. While the hydra wasn't attacking he made a quick sprint to his fallen bag and pulled out his lute from the sack on the ground. His fingers quickly got into place just in time to stop the snake in its tracks. A melody sweet and melancholic filled the air with intense vibrations. Soon, the music behind the song that Vygarast was playing, The Tomb of the Warrior, was lost in the drumming sound that echoed around him.

The ground under the snake started receding, the earth itself getting swept into a fearful melody of war. One of the songs written for combat, Vygarast was not so familiar with it. Even so, he knew that it was enough to kill. The ground beneath the hydra suddenly turned to mud and the creature sank into it until nothing was showing but the two writing heads. With a bitter twang of the lute and a mighty roar to end the song, the ground turned solid once again. Vygarast quickly retrieved his sword and carefully approached the hydra. He was careful to judge just how far the heads could attack, moving in slowly with his hands holding his sword above his head, ready for a killing strike. He taunted the beast with his sword, causing the heads to strike. He did this one last time, and as their where extended he moved in quickly with a powerful strike. The first head fell to the ground. When the remaining head came in to strike, he rolled under it and then chopped the last head off at the base with a mighty blow. Green blood spouted everywhere as Vygarast quickly cut every last piece of the hydra off that was above the ground. He stood there for many minutes, the gore running from his clothes and face, but he did not move until he was absolutely sure the monster would not regenerate. He has a battle rage in his veins the likes he had never felt before. He felt alive! He felt stronger.

Vygarast was in the middle of cleaning his sword in the grass when Azy landed on his shoulder again. This time, her touch was urgent... anxious.

We have to run Vygarast, if A Hydra is here, that means that also. . .

Her whispering suddenly stopped, as if a tall wall separated them. The small fairy tried to speak, but she couldn't.

"That means what Azy? What is going on?"

Vygarast would remember that sensation for the rest of his life; first sensing the corruption of his magic and then seeing the man jump out of the shadows from behind a tree trunk, a man walking on the other side of the river.

His voice was hoarse, deep, and steady. "Your friend probably meant to warn you of me, my young Bard. I greet you, half-elf of the forest mountains."

Chapter 6 : The Meddler and The Ogre

With a swift move, Vygarast brought up his sword. The man was standing on the other side of the river, but something inside the Bard's guts warned him that the distance was insignificant between them. He wanted to run, to get away and forget everything about saving his father. Still, his mind was set; he had to carry on.

"Oh, you're more daring than your fellow kind. I can sense great things coming from you, Bard, but not if you keep carrying on with this... fly on your shoulders." Even by standing on the other side of the river, his voice was heard clearly above the gurgle of the water.

"Leave Azore alone. Who are you? What do you want from us?" As Vygarast talked, the shadows around the cloaked man twisted around him, covering his face in the middle of the day. The only thing that Vygarast could tell from this distance was a pair of golden eyes, striking him with sneers of apathy before it disappeared into the shadows. The man was instantly almost invisible, lost in the forest somewhere.

"Azore? Oh, you mean the fairy? Maybe you have mistaken my intentions. I was doing you a favor, protecting you from this creature." The cloaked man walked up and down the river bank, using his hands to put emphasis on his words.

"What are you talking about? Azore is my friend and you're doing something to her mind, not letting her talk to me."

For a moment, Vygarast lost the man from his sight. "Fairies are sneaky creatures, Bard." He had suddenly appeared behind him, pinching the fairy's wings and lifting her in the air towards him. He continued, with Azy in his hand trying to get away. "Fairies offer you words of advice that in secret serve their own purposes. Do you think that their Queen," he uttered the word with disgust, as if not believing in the authority of the titled person, "gave a damn about you half-elves? Or us humans? The Immortal Creatures have only one purpose, and that is to keep being immortal. Don't forget that."

With his sword in hand, Vygarast tightened his grip on the hilt of his weapon, waiting for the right moment to strike. However, no matter what he did, his mind was refusing to give the order. *Who is this guy? How can he manipulate the light to his own will without using instruments?*

Vygarast, without thinking too strongly over it, took a step forward and swung his sword aiming at the man's exposed neck. What happened would haunt him for days; instead of cutting off the man's head, his sword stopped in mid-air, like it had hit a wall made of air. The man suddenly turned, and for a moment his golden eyes had lost every sense of logic. Vygarast sensed the man's blood lust. If it wasn't so plain to see that the man was actually a human, he would have mistaken him for a beast.

A tuft of red hair now licked the man's forehead. His hair had the color of the setting sun, the twilight red that reigned between night and day. Vygarast thought of backing away, but the air currents didn't let him move. The man slowly raised his hand to the same height as Vygarast's neck, and with his fingers tensing like claws; the Bard could feel his throat closing, to the point where he started to choke.

"You back-stabbing, dirty, half-breed, I tried to be reasonable with you and you chose the uncivilized half of your origin. If that is what you want, then so it will be," and with a disdainful expression on his face, he threw Azy away. Vygarast somehow wrenched free from the invisible grip on his neck and hurtled forward, catching her before she hit to the ground. A crackling sound echoing through the woods was the last thing that Vygarast heard before the man left in a flash.

Now that he was gone, Vygarast felt the air around him grow lighter, and the shadows of the trees receded to let the light pass. The Bard hadn't noticed that the man had made such a difference to everything around him, but gasping with Azy in his hands, Vygarast felt relieved he didn't have to fight him. His instruments were of no match for the man, at least not at his current level of training. However, something inside him warned him that not even a fully trained Bard would be enough to take down that man... and by the way he was talking, he was starting to think he wasn't a man at all.

Vygarast? Are you okay? Do you want me to heal you? Finally, the little fairy's voice was back to normal, like only just a moment of silent had passed by between them, but it felt like an eternity to Vygarast. He didn't realize until just that moment just how much he adored little Azy.

"Yes. I'm okay. How about you? Did he hurt you?"

The fairy didn't answer, but Vygarast caught a glimpse of her head shaking. He put her gently on his shoulder and the little fairy rested her back against his neck. *Thank the great Mother. Consider yourself very lucky young Bard, very lucky indeed. There are few people that get away alive when meeting with a Meddler.*

The title ringed a bell in Vygarast's mind, but still he couldn't quite remember the meaning behind the word. "A Meddler? I have heard about them before, but not much. Who are they?"

Meddlers are the name that people gave to people like him. We call them Darkens, humans taken by the corruption of the magic. A Darken is someone who can cast without instruments, making him a very dangerous and very bad creature, as doing this twists their souls to evil.

"Creature? Didn't you just say that Meddlers are humans?"

No, they are not anymore. After shedding away their humanity in order to be able to cast more powerful spells, Meddlers stopped feeding on fruits and meat, and started feeding on destiny itself. Darkens are indeed meddlers, but in a twisted, unimaginable way. They can sense the hidden potential of a person's destiny and by subtly driving them away from their path, they get stronger on what that person missed from his life. For example, imagine if a Meddler appeared and convinced a young man to not talk to the woman who could be the love of his life? The hidden potential of a destiny like that is tremendous, and Meddlers feed on that. What if that man was destined to be a mighty hero with the help of his new found love? The potential ramifications of events like these are immense! The lives of hundred, thousands or even hundreds of thousands can be influenced by these Meddlers of fate!

"So that's why they call them Meddlers. But why didn't he just kill me then? Wouldn't that waste my hidden potential?

It does not work like that. Your destiny is shaped around your own choices. If you're violently pushed into another direction, like if a Meddler killed you, your hidden potential would just vanish and the meddler would pay a heavy price from the hidden forces, while accomplishing nothing. Destiny would reset again as if nothing happened. They have to trick you into taking that choice by yourself. That is when they have won."

Vygarast took a long and tired sigh. After his battle with the Hydra and his meeting with the Meddler, he wanted to just rest. But he didn't have time to spare. The longer he waited, the more his father was in need of his help. "Even so, I can't let my father die because I was too tired to defend myself properly.

Azy gave him a quick kiss on the cheek. *Your destiny is still your own Vygarast. I'll help you beat this meddler. I am well versed in their games. I was taught by the queen of fairies herself! He just caught me off-guard. Now that I know he is around... I'll be ready next time.*

Vygarast felt sudden energy surge through him. "Thanks Azy!" Vygarast stated as he gathered up all his supplies and quickly ate some of his food rations. I have to kill that Ogre and find a way to get the wizard to help my father."

Vygarast strengthened his resolve and started to the other side of the river, where the Meddler walked mere moments before. He didn't know these parts all that well, but if the instructions the villagers gave him were true, then the Ogre's lair was close to the Wizard's Tower.

Throughout their short, silent walk, a thought echoed in Vygarast's mind. *What did he mean by saying that I followed the worst half of my origin? Did he mean the elves or the humans? And why he left when he could kill me? Is my fate that important?*

Lost in his thoughts, Vygarast almost stumbled on what it seemed like a bone on the ground. Startled by his sudden discovery, the Bard moved to one side and got ready for a fight. Before him he saw a long trail of bones and human skulls, going deeper into the woods.

Vygarast had thought that the Ogre would somehow be in a vulnerable position when he met it, making it easy for him to play his magic and trap it before slaughtering it. It was clear now that the beast did not have a specific lair, but wandered the deep part of the forest endlessly, feasting on its victims.

"Azy, what now? If we don't know where it is, then I have no chance against it. My whole plan has depended on catching it off guard."

Before he was able to complete his sentence, a slight tremor of the ground warned them, but by then it was too late to hide anymore. Vygarast drew his sword, only to feel a powerful force tossing him out three feet in the air to smash against the trunk of a giant elm tree. The roar that followed was that of a monster, sounding nothing like what Vygarast had heard before.

Oh great Mother, I had forgotten what the Ogres looked like, Azy whispered into Vygarast's mind. She floated close to the ground where Vygarast lay, trying to raise his morale, but the man was unable to even stand on his feet and his thoughts just pained her. She was not looking so great either. The glittering aura surrounding her flashed now and then, like the first night they met. If they had a chance to get out of this alive, they had to work together. Fortunately, they both thought the same thing.

I will distract him. Cast your most powerful spell at him, she said and flew away before Vygarast had time to protest.

Up until then, Vygarast had not even seen the monster before him. Now that he did, he realized that every song mentioning Ogres was not doing them justice. Tall like a house, with a wolfish fur covering his skin, and as wide as two men standing shoulder to shoulder, this Ogre looked like an overgrown bear. And then some.

Vygarast gasped, watching the monster. "How in the heck did this thing sneak up on me?" Then he realized... this was an ambush. A beautiful perfect path right up to the kill spot. For a moment he thought of running away, abandoning his quest. But, after hearing the monster talk, he felt his anger burn. Somewhere in his mind, he couldn't fathom that a creature like that could talk. "Master... told me... take care... of the elf... and the fairy." The sounds coming out of its mouth were crude, fitting its intimidating appearance.

Master? What could he mean...? Vygarast thought, but before he could get his answer, he saw Azy falling dangerously fast towards the ground. "Azore!!!" He bellowed, but it was too late. She hit the ground hard and stopped moving. The ogre chortled loudly and turned to face Vygarast.

"Your. . .turn," he growled and stomped his way towards Vygarast. The man knew that his magic would not work fast enough to immobilize it, and his sword would not be enough to cut it down.

What to do? What would Lanarast do if he was here? He jumped out of the ogre's way, trying to find steady footing against the monster. Towering above him, it was difficult to aim for a vital part, and he was sure that his skin would be tough. His eyes were dark red, and his mouth was half open revealing sharp teeth.

Think Vygarast! You can't keep dodging its attacks without a plan. There must be something you can do! Suddenly, a bright light caught his attention. It was building up fast, getting closer, actually surprising Vygarast. *What is this?* he thought.

As the little orb got closer, he was able to recognize the warm feeling coming from that light.

Without losing any time, Vygarast clenched the hilt of his sword in both hands tightly and got ready. The Ogre hadn't noticed Azy when the fairy blinded the giant with her powerful magic light. A sudden roar came from deep within his lungs as the towering giant rubbed his eyes, trying to reclaim his lost sight.

It staggered, ready to fall. Out of nowhere, Vygarast's feet started moving on their own, getting him closer and closer to the beast's own unsteady feet. With a sharp swing, he cut a deep wound at the Ogre's knee joint, making it roar in pain, and then fall on its back.

Amidst its roars, Vygarast climbed on its chest and put his sharp steel above its neck. The ugly Ogre, still half-blinded by Azy's sudden assault, could not focus on the enemy. Instead, it uttered: "Who... are... you?"

A deep rage coming from deep within Vygarast's guts drove him to press the steel of his sword into the Ogre's neck. "I ask the questions here. Who is your master? Who ordered you to attack us?"

"You... are... so big..." it muttered, the last words it would ever say, before a black shadow swallowed it whole. Vygarast was barely able to get away from the vile magic, doing a powerful back flip and landing in a crouched position.

For the first time after three long days, Vygarast couldn't keep his eyes open.

Chapter 7: The Owl Wizard

Vygarast woke up inside a dark, cool place, with a high ceiling. There were two spiraling staircases intertwining in what seemed like an elaborate dance of stonework. His head ached more than anything else in his body, the damp cold floor helping him recover more quickly. Everything was hazy in his mind, up to his fight with the Ogre. Abruptly, another memory came up to his mind.

"Azy? Azy, are you okay?" he said, quickly sitting on his butt and searching everywhere around him.

Yes, I'm right here. Don't stretch yourself. We're safe in here. But, even though she tried to reassure him, her talk was closely connected to her feelings, and in what it seemed like a stutter to a normal human, it felt like a warning coming from her.

"You! The marked one! You're finally awake!" A shrewd voice came from above, from where the two spiraling staircases met. A man, a really old man, stood there, with his white robe falling in waves all the way to the stony floor. As he descended, Vygarast was finally able to catch up with the unraveling events.

"Sir Wizard... I'm sorry. I didn't want to disturb you," even though he was still not sure how he ended up in there.

"Silence, child. A very important guest asked me to shelter you until you regained your consciousness. Now, if you excuse me esteemed fairy-child Azore, I'll have to ask you to leave. I have just woken up from my slumber, and this half-breed did not come prepared."

For the first time after meeting Azore, Vygarast heard what it was probably her true voice. In one of their late night talks, Azy had mentioned that talking straight to his mind was the only way they could communicate. Her language was too complex for a mere half-elf and could only be uttered at the Fairy Kingdom, or in places of diplomatic importance. That happened because a fairy could not lie if she used her native language.

Now that Vygarast heard her voice herself, it was like a wave of sadness touched his very soul. A vowel-centered language, full of ups and downs, and sudden turns in tone, seemed like a heart-felt sample of what was an ancient relic. When she ended, the wizard was standing still on the last step of the stairway, his hands behind his back.

Seeing him up close, Vygarast finally understood why he was called the Owl-Wizard. His eyes were bigger than average, and the skin around them was plagued by dark circles. It was like a constant shadow was falling on his face; his long, white beard almost licked the floor, and his fingers were scrawny and sinewy.

"Is that Passing creature so important for one of the Immortal races? I can help you with the Dukes. I can take us to them at a moment's notice and make them sign your treaty. Why use him?"

And then, the voice came again. This time it was faster, flowing like a river in early spring, just after the first snows of the mountains started melting. Fortunately, her speech was short.

"Fine. If that is your wish, then so be it. But remember, the rules are the rules. I will overlook the price, but he still has to prove he's charismatic and intelligent. I'm done helping creatures with dark intentions."

Again, he was confused. The tale told of a greedy Wizard, one who would not help anyone without 1001 gold coins. But Azy had seemed to persuade him without gold. What did she say to him?

Still wondering, he felt a gust of air carry him upright. "Up, up boy. Consider yourself lucky that one of the fairies favors you. This will happen once, and only once. You have to answer my riddle to earn my help. People that are charismatic are usually intelligent and answering my riddle will prove you're both. So, are you ready boy?" But before Vygarast had time to reply, the Wizard started talking:

"I never was, am always to be,
No one ever saw me, nor ever will
And yet I am the confidence of all
To live and breathe on this terrestrial ball."

His booming voice filled the whole tower, making Vygarast ready to back off from this crazy man. Vygarast knew he had heard the riddle before, but he was not sure. His father always talked with riddles, especially when he was with Lanarast the Bold, but Vygarast never gave them enough attention, thinking them talk for old men.

Think! Think! Never was, always to be. . .no one saw me, nor ever will. . . damn, who am I kidding? I don't know. With a quick glance he found the warm light emanating from Azy. She had showed such trust to him, and he was not able to solve a small riddle.

He decided to follow his gut and tell the first thing it popped up in his mind. "Maybe... is it a child?"

The Wizard raised his brows but never seemed to change his expression. "You're wrong, marked one. Children younger than you were able to solve this riddle in the past, but it seems that your kind has lost much in knowledge. The correct answer is the future, boy. Remember that as your future is afflicted with bad luck."

And without an expression on his face, the Wizard turned and started going up to the staircase again. Lost in disbelief, Vygarast could not control his emotions. "Wait! Wait! I'll do anything to save my father. Just name your price and I'll bring that much gold, and two times more. Just wait!"

The Wizard was now half way towards the top. *Stupid Vygarast! You have to do something! Use your head!* And just like that, a memory popped from deep within.

His master, Lanarast the Bold, had taught every single student of his the same things exactly. The first lesson was held up the first day of Autumn, outside the training grounds. He always gathered his new students around, as well as the older ones, and instructed them on what it means to be a Bard.

"Bards are not just playing the flute and casting spells. Being a Bard is to be constantly in love with music, no matter where it comes from. Music itself is magic, one able to soothe even the hardest of hearts. Don't forget that! Your power does not lie in being strong casters, but using your heads and singing. Solve your problems with charisma and a wide grin on your faces."

And just like that, Vygarast dug up the lute from his leather bag and squatted on the floor. He picked up the first song that came to his head, a lullaby of the elves that his mother used to sing to him when he was just a child. The melody was still hazy in his mind when he started, but as the notes took a hold of his hands, he was able to recite the whole song by heart.

He hadn't sang like that before, not even to impress a girl, or show off to the rest of his friends. This time, Vygarast was singing of his love for his father. When he started, he didn't expect for the old Wizard to stop. Maybe he wished really hard for it, or wanted to make a miracle out of thin air, but he didn't expect it. As the song went on, even Vygarast himself forgot for a second that he was standing in an old, wizard's tower somewhere West of Crowfair.

For a short moment, he was watching his mother leave again, with tears running down his face. When the song ended, his eyes were wet, but he managed to hold them back.

A pair of clapping hands surprised him. "That was beautiful, boy, a little too melancholic for my tastes, but beautiful nevertheless. I will help you, Vygarast the Bard, but only because your charisma greatly transcends your wits. And if the fairy Queen is right indeed, you're more needed with aiding Azore than mourning your dead father. Come... we have no time to lose."

And just like that, in a blink of the eye, they appeared just outside his house back in Midvein. He was suddenly home.

The wizard clapped his hands together and there was a mighty boom! He then commanded Vygarast to play the most victorious ballad he knew, and then enhanced his volume by tenfold! Azy hummed along in his head as he played the ballad of the mighty hero Kelyk who defended the realm with three heroes, five hundred archers and towers of stone! It wasn't long before they had a group of fifty people following them to Vygarast's home.

Lanarast was waiting outside his house, a look of disbelief on his face... quickly turning to a giant smile! He quickly embraced his young pupil and opened the door to allow the wizard inside.

The Owl Wizard frowned when he looked at Ornsell's sleeping body. "I should of charged the gold for this one." he stated sullenly. "Didn't realize it was so bad!" "He continued to whine for several minutes... giving unhappy looks to both Vygarast and Azy. "I'll be exhausted for six months after this! You realize?" he whines some more. But with all the people outside and crowding around the old wizard knew his reputation would be ruined if he didn't perform. With a sharp grimace... knowing the pain that was about to come... the Owl Wizard pulled out his gem of power and a ragged looking scroll. With a mighty stamp of his staff he began to chant. The air around the village suddenly changed, as if it was about to storm, and the villagers fell silent. All that could be heard was the booming voice of the owl wizard as it took on an unearthly tone.

Thunderclouds gathered and lightning danced about as the old wizard chanted and chanted in what seemed like hours, but was only thirty minutes. There was a final lightning strike followed by a deafening boom and a blinding red light. The wizard fell to his knees and Ornsell jumped to his feet, a crazed look in his eyes.

The feast that followed the lifting of the curse was the biggest that Vygarast had seen in many years. Ornsell, his father, was beloved by everyone in the village, but there was also another reason for them to celebrate. Vygarast had returned a hero. Even more than that, he brought news about the rising of the legends.

Ornsell was in the middle of the feasting, eating enough food to satisfy three men and surrounded by his lifelong friends. The Wizard had said little after lifting the curse, and pretended like he was ok, but Azy had whispered the truth to him. The wizard had sacrificed ten years of his life for that spell and barely survived. It was up to her to repay that debt now.

"His body will rush to regain its strength, so don't worry if he'll eat more than expected in the coming days. The curse cast to him was a strong one, probably coming from one of the Royal members of the harpies. If I had to guess, the Queen would be the only one powerful enough to do something like that, but we will never know for sure. Your father is safe, but tell him not to return to the forest, not until the harpy threat has been dealt with."

Vygarast nodded, feeling like a student once again. However, he had some questions himself. "What do you know of the Meddlers, great Wizard?"

"I know that they are people, humans mostly, that have defiled the sacred art of casting by using their dirty hands to draw from the flaws. You are a Bard, using instruments and flowing the magic through your art, but they are not anything like that. They have sacrificed their souls. Other than that, I don't know why he was there, and what he was doing. But this is not good. If I were to guess… then it is that you have a powerful destiny. Someone whose life course will affect many. Meddlers tend not meddle with those who do not matter."

After that, the Wizard took care of some things with Azore, and then vanished as quickly as he appeared, no doubt to recover as quickly as he could.

Everything moved so fast that Vygarast almost forgot about his promise to Azy.

When the crowd around his father thinned a bit, his son approached him. "Strong as a horse, tough as a rock, right?"

"And stubborn as a mule! Vygarast, my son, my savior." He said as he stood up and grabbed Vygarast and hugged him for like the tenth time this day. He was a bit full in the wine at this point and glad to be alive! Vygarast hadn't minded before, but he was serious now, so he demanded his father's attention. Somehow, Ornsell picked up on his son's mood. "Is something wrong my son? Is your wine sour?"

"No, no my father. I just promised something to Azy, and… and…," he stuttered.

"And you have to go. Yes, I figured that much. I might not be accustomed with all that creature talk yet, but there was no reason for a fairy to stay at our house if she didn't want something with you. Don't worry son. I knew that the time for you to travel the world was near, but it seemed that it was closer than I thought, right? I just wanted to enjoy every second with you that I can with you while I can."

The young Bard nodded. He didn't want to admit it, but he would miss his father. However, after talking a bit with him, Vygarast felt it even more than before, that anticipation of the trip, the time before a grand adventure would begin. He was Vygarast the Bard, and apparently his destiny was important indeed! He did not feel tired after all his ordeals and the price the old wizard had just paid for his father made him feel indebted.

Deep in the shadows somewhere in Midvein a dark voice filled with hate stated in a snarl: "I hate that happy music, and that disgusting smell of victory on those humans. But it seems that I was right about the young Bard. His destiny changed while battling Bikor the Ogre, and now he's even now more tasty than before. If only I could catch him without that damned fairy flying around him. "

The Meddler was hiding behind one of the houses of Midvein. He didn't want to be seen, not when his own master ordered him to stay put and hide. He was, after all, under strict orders to just watch and not act. With a quick movement of his hands and a wide smile on his face, the red-haired man disappeared in thin air. The first part of his plan was successful and he was going to collect his reward!

The End of Book 1

Thanks for purchasing this book and be sure to check out the excitement in Book 2 of The Bard's Tale Series to see what happens next. It will be coming out soon.

Sneak Preview of The Angel's Blessing

Chapter 1 The Day of the White Rook

My Master did not become the great Warrior Shaman of peace because he was born with the blessings of the gods. He did not rise to his exalted place in the history of our worlds by the chance of ancestry, nor was he a child of fortune. He had no advantage other than his cunning, and he had no blessing other than that given to him by his grandfather. And that blessing was herb-lore.

My master was conceived and born in violence.

His mother was a young beauty who was ravaged by the invading Veylus pirates when our beloved city of Barnacle Atoll was overrun. When her time to give birth came, she held the newborn infant to her breast, the scrawny infant seeking to suckle a tit. But the nipple that the child found was cold and so he turned to his grandfather's thumb instead, and that thumb was hard and calloused and yet rich with the taste of mother-earth and her herbs. And so in his first suckle of life, the babe that was to be known simply as Kell, tasted the roots of us all.

Kell spent his youngest years under the domination of the brigands, and he quickly learned stealth and cunning as a way of life. In time, the Veylus were ousted by the armada of Queen Anastasias, and while her liberation was near devastation, the people of the Barnacles were once again free. With that freedom came years of reconstruction and tribute to the Queen, but that was far better than the pirates.

In that time Kell grew up as boys will. He was astounded with the world. His grandfather had a bountiful garden, and in there Kell saw crawlers and wigglers and flyers of all sorts. As a toddler, he tasted them and found them much crunchier than the wiggly ones of the root cellar. His grandfather often looked at him and sighed as adults will. But despite his odd tastes, he grew up healthy and strong.

Their small island of Dunsil wasn't on many sea-routes, but he and his grandfather were often visited by passing ships looking for a remedy to help a wounded or sick crewman. Often a boatful of sailors would come ashore and seek one of grandfather's special elixirs, and then ask of the ways with which to work the earth's gift. His grandfather never refused anyone in need -- for a fair price. Over the years, the legends grew of his incredible remedies. It was an ideal childhood and Kell was very happy.

Until the day that the Dorimans engulfed their island.

They were a gang of thugs with ships. Their fleet was small and fast and they would prey on defenseless lands, not to conquer, but to plunder and destroy. And before the Queen's forces could come to aid, they would sail away into the night's fog only to reappear in some other land, rough-handed and demanding. They wore no uniforms, and in their motley gear Kell saw them as something to be afraid of. He was a teenager at the time and the Dorimans saw him as a value to their number. And so at his grandfather's urging, he drew on all his cunning and he ran away.

He ran across the crest of the island and to the common ground where others were also gathering and afraid. Understanding his plight, the elders brought him to a cove with a light boat hidden within. They told him to sail straight to Angove's Cay, which was the home of Wendfala the Witch.

The young witch, seeing my Master's comely and youthful state, took him in and proceeded to teach him the ancient ways. It is said that in those dark hours while our very island writhed beneath the boots of the Dorimans, Wendfala made my Master into a man, and the young boy emerged from her clutches alert, able and with a new sort of strength that radiated off him like an aura.

They say that he emerged from her embraces as a magical paladin who single-handedly rallied the people and sent the Dorimans howling away and afraid. They say that he was the hero who liberated our islands and that the Doriman still fear his name. And they say that when he was done with the Dorimans, the of battle was still upon him, and so he sailed the world in search of glory, wisdom and to inflict Holy Justice upon the wicked. For years sailors and merchants would land on our island and tell tales of Kell's valor in lands unknown.

That's what they say.

In the years of peace that followed many tales were told and retold, and then told and changed again and again. And in the small confines of the island of Dunsil the simple herbalist's grandchild became a living legend.

He returned to our island the year that I was born, and while many looked at the legendary hero in awe, their real amazement was that the lad looked as if he had never left. It was as though time had not touched him, and when he walked into his grandfather's cottage with his backpack full of magic and treasures, the old man simply looked up and told him that the garden needed tending.

He would say nothing of his adventures, but people would talk. Kell shunned their stories, but he didn't shun their company. He was still young and he had a quick wit at the tavern and loved winning at darts and skittles. The young women all eyed him and so at the festivals and dances he never lacked a partner. His knowledge of herbs and medicines grew as his grandfather taught him all he knew as he waned in years. People came to trust the young man as they did his old grandfather, sometimes more.

In time, the great herbalist finally passed. Every man woman and child on Dunsil stood on the white sands of the island's eastern shore as Kell made ready the last boat. They covered his body in beautiful flower blossoms, in hopes that the sea would pause and delight in the scent and so allow fair winds to carry him to his eternal paradise. Even the witch Wendfala came to give her blessing.

I was just a small boy at the time. I remember my mother urging me, my sisters and my brothers to let go of our flowers. But I was fascinated by the naked old man. He was nothing but old bones wrapped in tan skin at the bottom of a small rustic boat, and yet the blossoms made him seem almost alive.

"Forgive my child Kell," my mother said. "He is –"

"Young," Kell said. "And fascinated."

Then he set his gaze on me and he smiled.

It was not that long after the funeral that I was selected to be Kell's apprentice. I trembled with the honor and surged with excitement.

I had heard all of the grand tales. Indeed, I had been raised in the shadow of those magnificent stories, and when he and my father bartered for my apprenticeship, I thought that the gods themselves had blessed me.

"He's kind of scrawny."

"Yeah," my father said. "He is. But how much bulk do you need to scratch out your herbs?"

Kell frowned.

"Look," my father said. "I have a farm. Farming is a strong man's job. The boy will be better in your hands. I will give you milk, cheese and all the whey you want for four years."

"Seven."

I listened as they haggled over my worth. In the end I went for the price of six years of milk, three of cheeses and all the whey I could carry between the houses until I was seventeen.

It was a good bargain.

Master Kell was a soft-spoken and kindly man. He treated me well and our house wanted for nothing. Along with teaching me herb lore, he also taught me numbers and letters, and while I found numbers valuable in weighing and mixing and figuring out the price to put on a remedy, I never understood why Kell put so much value on writing.

We worked in a daily routine and there were always things to get done or learn. But Kell was a light-hearted soul and we often took the time to play. We would sometimes end a long day frolicking and fishing on one side of Crystal Lake while the women washed their laundry on the other. My master had an eye for the ladies and there were quite a few nights that I spent alone sleeping under the Starlight.

When I came into my teenage years I learned two very important lessons of life. One was girls. When I was young girls were simply giggly playmates, but as I matured I began to see those gigglers grow round, soft and firm, and that made me wonder. And there were odd things about my own body that I didn't understand; strange stirrings and desires. I asked my master about these feelings but he seemed somewhat at a loss, then smiled and assured me that all would be revealed in time.

I wondered about how long that time might be. And then one day a woman named Loleena came calling. She was from the other side of the island and I barely knew her. Kell graciously invited her to sup with us and the woman seemed to take an immediate interest in me. I was flattered that such a fine lady would even recognize my existence, let along talk with me.

The night was cool and getting cooler. Kell excused himself to gather more wood for the fire, but he didn't return till dawn. And that night Loleena helped me understand what it was like to be a man.

Over time I became an expert at herb lore and my master's special elixirs where in high demand, giving me plenty of practice at the craft. When it came time for the harvest festival, I was invited for the first time to join the adults around the big bonfire. There was music and dancing, and everyone cheered when Kell produced a keg of his special brew. The draught was sweet and heady and at first I didn't feel its effects. But then the festival started to feel a lot more happier to me. The dancing was lighter, the music was sweeter, and the young girls seemed prettier. The brew seemed to have the same effect on the girls as well, because they suddenly found me handsome. I did not lack for sweet company all that day and night.

Winters on the Atoll were usually cold and dreary. Work still needed to be done, but the sun would set earlier and earlier and the nights cooped up in the cottage could be wearisome. In those days I was glad to have learned my letters. My master had books on his craft and a boring volume entitled *The List of Leaves* that helped pass the dreary time.

We woke one chill sunny morning to a racket outside. Rooks were calling and crying. We rushed outside to see what was happening and the sky was nearly blotted out by their numbers. It was an amazing sight. Thousands of them were circling overhead. They seemed to be whirling in a vortex that narrowed closer and closer to the center eye, and in that eye I saw a single speck of white.

As we watched the birds became more and more frantic. The center mass of birds began to dip down and then formed into a funnel. I cried out and fell back to shield myself, but when they were only a few hundred feet above us a single rook parted from the myriad, spread its massive wings and began to descend. As it got closer we could see that the rook was as white as snow.

The pearlescent feathers seemed almost to gleam and its beak was like polished marble, but even as its spiny claws touched the sand of the earth the creature transformed. There stood before us a tall, bald man with skin as black as the night that seemed to almost shine blue where the sunlight fell on it. He was hairless from his head to his eyebrows and everywhere else a man should have hair. But what truly astonished me was that there was no manhood. At the place where his thighs met his pelvis there was nothing but smooth dark flesh.

"You are Kell," the man said in a silky, almost liquid voice.

"I am."

And for all of my amazement and growing fear my master was as calm as the sea on a spring morning.

"I am an emissary from Wendfala," he said. "The Witch calls on your pledge."

There was a long pause before my master spoke. The birds above had wheeled out in a huge circle letting the sun shine onto us.

"Why doesn't Wendfala come herself to call on this sacred pledge?" Kell asked in a powerful voice.

"She has been kidnapped," the man-bird said.

"Kidnapped?" Kell bellowed, his hand unconsciously flexing as if to grab his weapon.

"She needs your help. In fact the whole of the Nine domains need your help."

"With what? What is going on?" Kell asked with obvious concern in his voice.

"Wendfala calls for you. It's not for me to judge her choice. I am only a messenger and ask you to hear her plea. I see smoke from your chimney. Can we go inside? It's cold out here without feathers."

"Um, sure. But first tell me, what is your name?" said Kell

"I am Byrinius."

Kell motioned towards his house and as they turned to go inside Byrinius pointed towards me and asked who I was.

"This is Longo Nonan," Kell said. "He is my apprentice."

"Longo," the man said. "Look at me boy. I have no hair and I have nothing where a human male should have something. But can you tell me what else there is about me that is not like you?"

At first I was frightened and my brain refused to work. But it felt as though the two would stare at me until I either flushed or fumbled like a child, or I solved the riddle. I looked. Then I looked again, and then I saw, but the words would not form and so I simply pointed to my belly.

"That's right," Byrinius said laughing long and hard. "I have no naval. I was not born, I was hatched. Kell, the lad is astute. Let him come with us and listen."

My master gave me a strange look, but I went with them and sat quietly in the corner. Kell offered tea but the man refused. He plucked a large ember from the fire, sat at the table, and held the glowing thing in his palm as he spoke.

"Visalth is coming," the man said.

As he spoke, vapors rose from the glowing ember. The smoke grew a little and then began to spin, then gather and spread into a wide sphere, and in the center of the sphere an image began to form. It was the image of a giant skeletal Dragon... A Bone Dragon.

I had heard of such things in stories, and in my youth they were terrifying. The mindless, soulless things would always seek to steal, kill and destroy and they could listen to no reason and had no fear for their own lives.

But these were modern times. Such myths were put away long ago along with frost fairies and trolls.

But that day my eyes had seen a bird transform into the vestige of a man who was now holding a scorching cinder in his hand as if it were a pebble, and the vision that formed in the room made me believe.

The dragon's bones were not like the white bleached things of men I had seen washed up on the beaches. They were deep brown like rotten teeth. It's long skull was swept back, flaring out into nine horns that turned forward like barbed fish-hooks. The hollow orbits were long, narrow and without eyes. It had a look of evil about it. I could not count the many spike-tipped vertebrae of the creature's neck, but the thing could wind and twist like a snake. Its ribs were slender, but what once had been the torso was long. Its fore-limbs grew from a solid breast-plate that looked scarred and beaten, and they were like a man's arms ending in grasping fingers. Its massive hind-legs bent like a deer, but the thighs could have been as thick as a trader ship's mast, and the claws could have crushed our house. The wings that sprouted from its back spread like enormous bird fingers, but between those bones there was no skin, only what looked like remnants of tattered sails or the clinging bits of flesh from creatures undreamed. The tail of the beast was easily as long as the whole creature, and as I watched the dragon fly about in the vision, the bony tail would whip back between the wings to attack like a scorpion.

"Magnificent," Kell said. "Truly a feat of powerful magic."

"Dark magic," Byrinius replied.

We watched the scene as the dragon lay waste to a solid castle set on a hill. The land was unknown to me. It was a lush place with rolling green grass, well cultivated farm land surrounded by walls and then a deep forest. But as we watched, the beast seemed to delight in wreaking ruin on the castle walls and buildings. An army of warriors looked helpless against the skeletal foe. Their arrows and bolts would bounce off the bones or sail through the empty spaces of its ribs. Even the catapults the men managed to muster had little effect, and they were quickly destroyed. When the undead horror had reduced the defenses to rubble it then turned on the army, sweeping men and cavalry away with its deadly tail.

"It seems bent on wanton destruction," Kell said.

"Not so. There is method in its madness. Observe."

I watched with a dull growing terror. When the army had been broken and the warriors were fleeing, men began to march in from the woods. The dragon seemed to suddenly heed some sort of call. It lifted and flew up on wings that were no wings, circling the walled city as the invaders easily took over.

"What are we seeing?" Kell asked. "What place is this?"

"It's Breakstone Hold, the Castle of Duke Venyez in Estile."

"Estile? That's in the Nine."

"It is," the man said. "It is on the Queen's western realms. The bone dragon's name is Visalth, and it's forces seem to be working their way along the alliance. Before Estile, the Duchy of Halnn fell. But the curious thing about the invasion is the pattern of assault. There is no warning, but just before an invasion all magic seems to disappear."

"What?"

"Wizards," the man went on, "witches, mages, even holy paladins seem to disappear. Whether these are physical or spiritual abductions I cannot say. But I do know that when Visalth appears there are none who can stand before him — they all disappear or get destroyed. And now Wendfala is captured, and from her prison she sends me to you ahead of the storm to get your aid."

Kell gulped his tea. The mystical scene vanished but Byrinius still held the glowing ember. My master stood and paced the room. He ran his fingers through his hair again and again. Then he finally stood before the window and gazed out to sea. He stood a long time. He then seemed decisive and strode to a locked wardrobe. He held his fingers over the handle and mumbled a quick verse. The doors popped open and from the inside he drew out a long and stout war-hammer that was glowing brightly.

The weapon was easily as long as my arm. Its handle was wrapped with red leather that showed stains of wear and sweat. The oaken shaft was carved in a hexagon. Cold blue steel ran from the crown down that shaft and was bolted with iron. The broad, flat head could easily have crushed an Ogres Skull, and the opposite side of the hammer was a nasty six sided piece of magical steel ending in a sharp point. The pommel was thick and ended with an 8 inch long double-bladed knife made of Admantium with a magically sharpened blade. Kell tossed his trusty weapon onto the table and the weight of it shook the table and dented it in several places.

"This is my little friend Ashrune," my master said. "How might we help?"

"You need to Flee this place." Byrinius said in a grave and urgent tone.

"Never! I will not run when my Queen's lands are in danger. I am no coward." Kell bellowed, outrage in his voice.

"Bravery in the face of such a monster is suicide," Byrinius said calmly. "The power behind Visalth is cunning, and so you must be just as crafty. Ashrune may be a noble weapon but even with the might of a Titan behind, it would barely scratch the creature's skull before you were impaled. You need something far mightier, and to find such a thing you need help that is beyond simple magic. You need an Angel."

Check out the rest of the story in book or audio book format on my website: www.LordHartRules.com

My Other Books and Audio Books

For A Special Treat, check out my

AUDIO BOOKS

THE ANGEL'S BLESSING
HOLY PALADIN'S QUEST
BLAINE HART

THE SANDS OF TIME
THE ANGEL'S BLESSING
BLAINE HART

Epic Fantasy Adventure
SPELL MASTER
WIZARD'S QUEST
BLAINE HART

TOWERS
Blaine Hart

Blaine Hart
The Bard's Tale
A Mysterious Journey

Thanks for reading!

If you enjoyed this book a nice review would be greatly appreciated.

Check Out all My Books and Audio Books at:
<u>www.LordHartRules.com</u>

9 781640 480971